"What is history?" the great nineteenth-century French author Alexandre Dumas once asked. "It is the nail on which I hang my novels." Indeed, the nail on which Dumas hung **The Count of Monte Cristo** involved an actual criminal case. Dumas, "elevating history to the dignity of the novel," fleshed out the real-life narrative, added a number of plot devices (including a hair's-breadth escape, an intriguing mystery, and a number of duels), and created a superb cast of supporting characters. Like several of his other works, the novel was first printed in serialized newspaper installments. By the time **The Count of Monte Cristo** appeared in 1844-45, Dumas already was among France's most popular authors, having perfected his melodramatic style in a series of highly successful plays and novels, including *The Three Musketeers*. Although celebrated by the public, **The Count of Monte Cristo** was viewed with disfavor by critics. Certainly, the novel has its literary weaknesses: the characters are overly simple, either good or evil; the story abounds in implausibilities; speech tends to be stilted and theatrical; there is a perplexing overabundance of secondary characters; calamity follows calamity, among them stabbings, poisonings, kidnappings, near-suicides, and much swordplay; and, finally, too much turns on fortuitous chance. In addition, his detractors charged Dumas — who often worked with collaborators — with running a novel factory; referring to Dumas' 301-volume *Complete Works,* one critic remarked, "No one has read *all* of Dumas — that would be as impossible as for him to have written it." However, since all of his manuscripts are in his own handwriting, it is now generally recognized that Dumas' aides provided only research and rough outlines. Later reassessments have muted some of the early criticism and, today, **The Count of Monte Cristo** — as popular with readers as ever — is regarded as a spellbinding adventure tale and a window into a dazzling era.

The Count of Monte Cristo
Classics Illustrated, Number 7

Wade Roberts, Editorial Director
Alex Wald, Art Director
Mike McCormick, Production Manager

PRINTING HISTORY
1st edition published April 1990

Copyright © 1990 by The Berkley Publishing Group and First Publishing, Inc. All rights reserved. No part of this book may be reproduced or transmitted in any form or by any means, electronic or mechanical, including photocopying, recording, or by information storage and retrieval system, without express written permission from the publishers.

For information, address: First Publishing, Inc., 435 North LaSalle St., Chicago, Illinois 60610.

ISBN 0-425-12028-7

TRADEMARK NOTICE: Classics Illustrated® is a registered trademark of Frawley Corporation. The Classics Illustrated logo is a trademark of The Berkley Publishing Group, Inc. and First Publishing, Inc. "Berkley" and the stylized "B" are trademarks of the Berkley Publishing Group. "First Publishing" and the stylized "1F" are trademarks of First Publishing, Inc.

Distributed by Berkley Sales & Marketing, a division of The Berkley Publishing Group, 200 Madison Avenue, New York, New York 10016.

Printed in the United States of America
1 2 3 4 5 6 7 8 9 0

MEMORIES WERE HIS ONLY POSSESSIONS NOW. MONSIEUR MORREL, THE SHIP'S OWNER, WHO PROMOTED HIM TO CAPTAINCY...

DANGLARS, THE FIRST MATE, A FERRET OF A MAN. HAD HE EXPECTED THE CAPTAINCY? HAD HE HANDED DANTÈS TO THE POLICE?

THE LOVELY MERCÉDÈS, HIS FIANCÉE-- AND IT WAS ON HER FACE THE MEMORIES ALWAYS STOPPED, AS DANTÈS' HEART BROKE...

HOW HAD HE ENDED HERE? THE PROSECUTOR, VILLEFORT, HAD THOUGHT DANTÈS INNOCENT...

NO!

THEN THE LETTER WAS MENTIONED... THAT DAMNED LETTER FROM ELBA, ISLAND HOME OF THE EXILED NAPOLEON...

I WILL NOT LIVE THIS WAY! I AM A MAN-- *A MAN!*

BETTER I SHOULD STARVE MYSELF TO DEATH THAN TO EXIST AS SOME CAPTURED, FORGOTTEN BEAST!

MY DEAREST MERCÉDÈS...IF ONLY...

WHAT--?!

SKRICH SKRICH

2

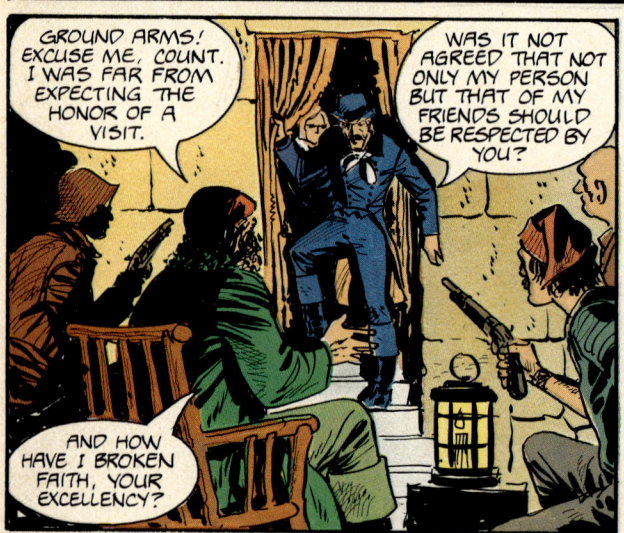

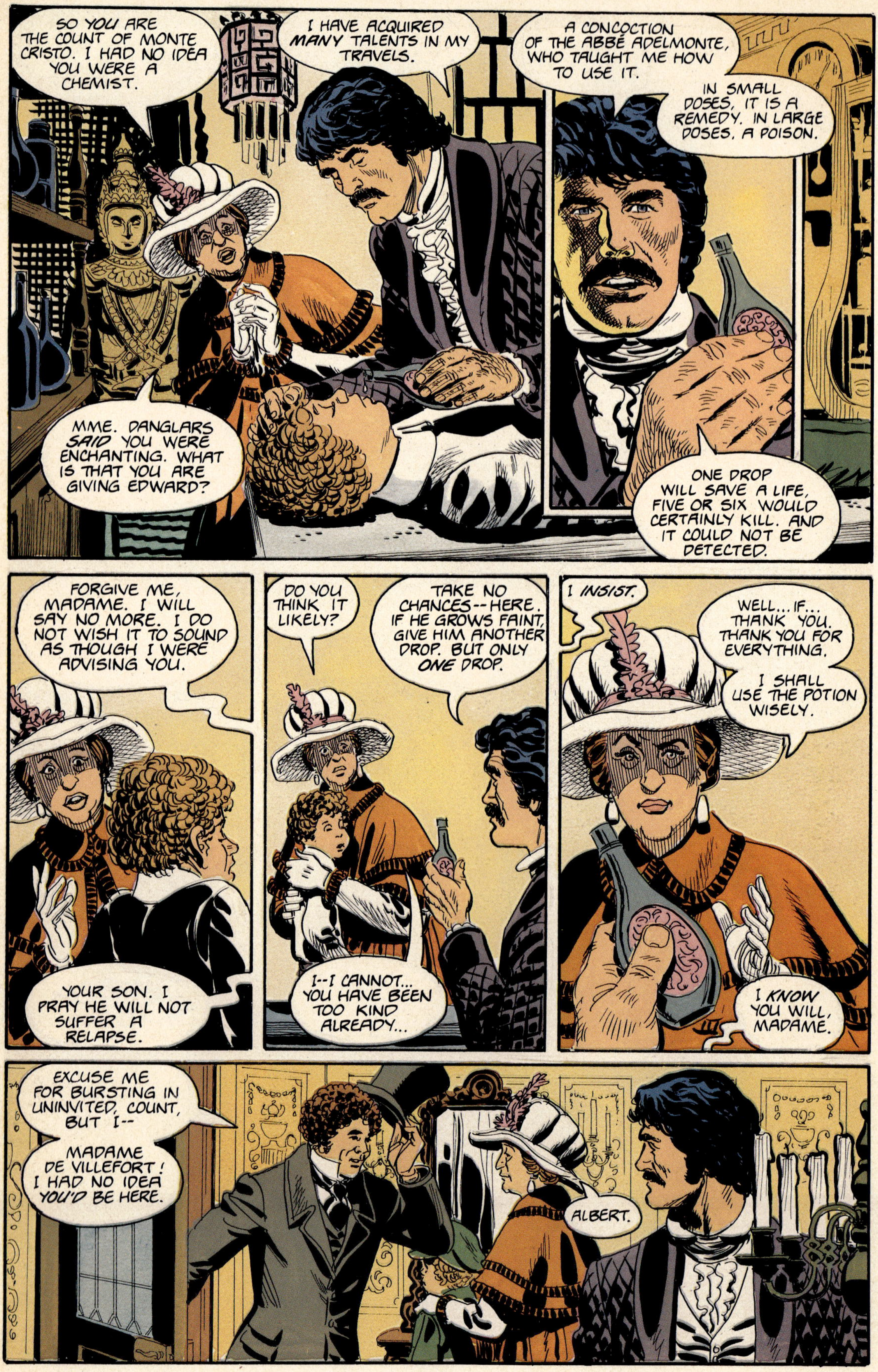

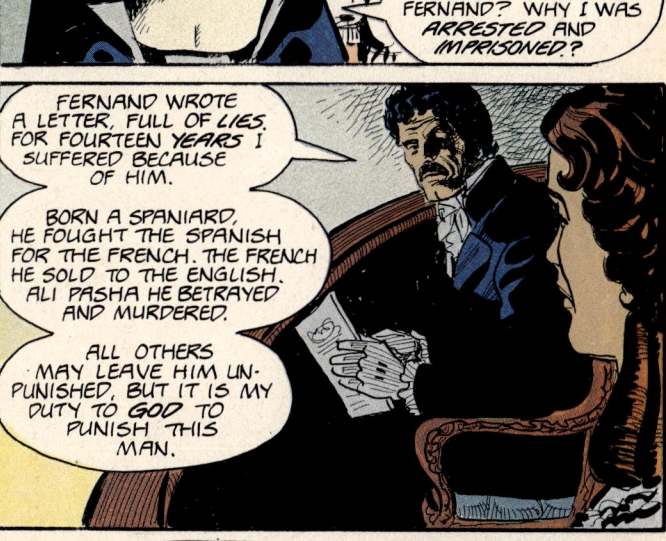

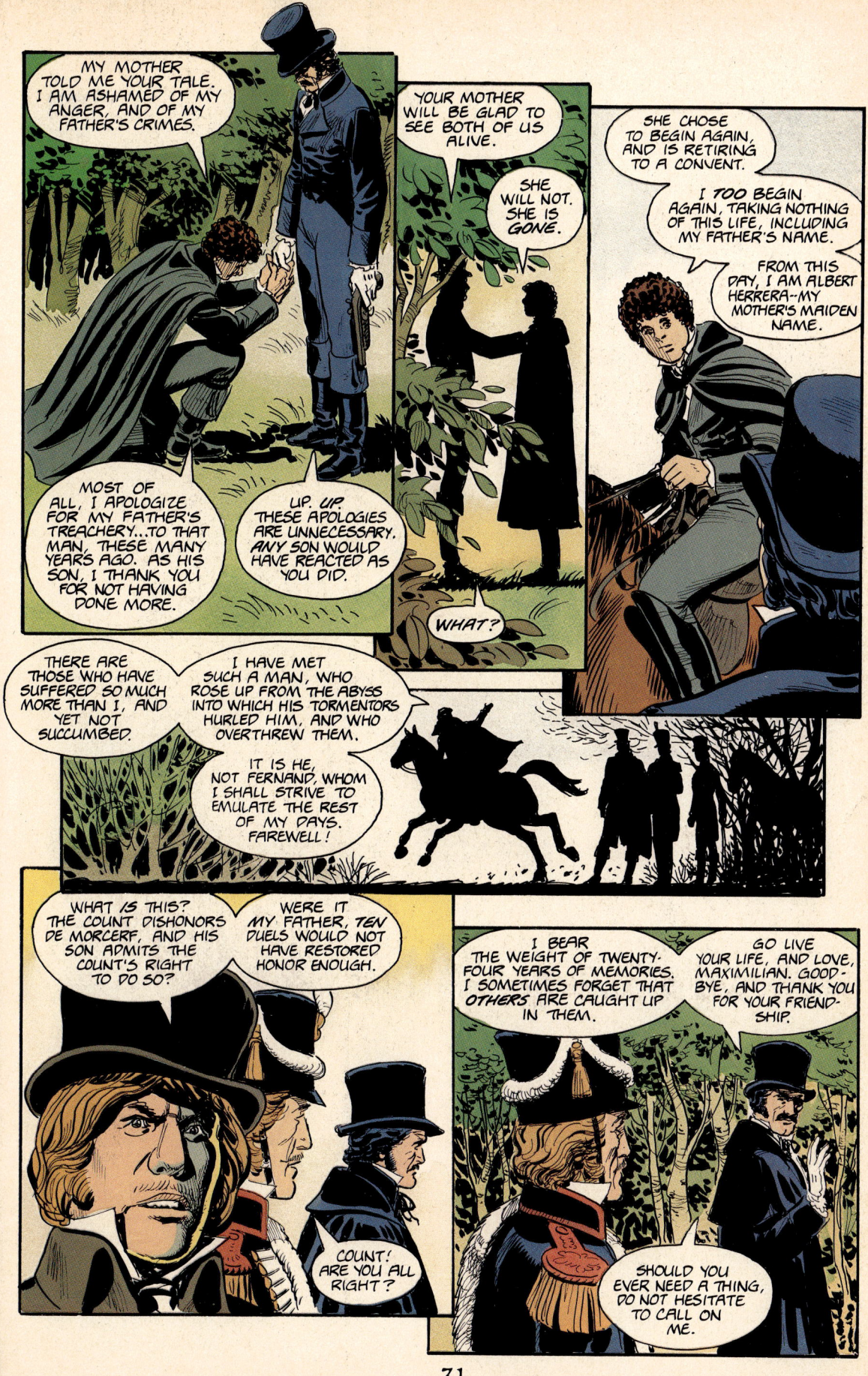

35

Alexandre Dumas was born in Villers-Cotterets, France, on July 24, 1802, the son of a mulatto general who had fought alongside Napoleon. General Dumas, however, fell out of favor with the French emperor, and died virtually penniless. Young Dumas' education was limited, but, upon his move to Paris in 1823, his graceful handwriting brought him a job in the secretariat of the Duc d'Orleans, later the King of France. In 1824, he fathered a son known as Alexandre Dumas *fils* (who also became a successful novelist and playwright). Dumas' first play, *Henri III et sa Cour* (1829), opened at the Comédie-Française before an enthusiastic audience. He achieved further fame with other theatrical triumphs: *Antony* (1831), *La Tour de Nesle* (1832), and *Kean* (1836). Dumas' grand, melodramatic historical romances began to appear around 1840, as serialized newspaper installments that were later collected into books. To assist in research, Dumas assembled a number of collaborators to create what he called his "factory." They combed newspapers, magazines, and books for suitably exciting plots, a practice that exposed Dumas to charges of pilfering history and pilfering from other writers. Also, Dumas' works were so massive and appeared with such rapidity that critics began to suspect they had been ghostwritten. Even had the accusations been proven, it is unlikely that French readers would have taken notice: Dumas' books were among the best-sellers of the time. The successes of *The Three Musketeers* (1844-1845), *Twenty Years After* (1845), *The Count of Monte Cristo* (1844), and *The Man in the Iron Mask* (1848-1850) brought Dumas wealth as well as glory. In 1848, Dumas married his mistress, Ida Ferrier, and built his own Château de Monte Cristo; more than 600 attended the housewarming dinner. Flamboyant and reckless, Dumas spent with abandon, socializing with royalty and the elite of Paris. Soon bankrupt, he fled to Belgium in 1851 to escape creditors. Dumas died on December 5, 1870; ever-romantic, he said of death, "I shall tell her a story, and she will be kind to me."

Dan Spiegle was born in Washington state in 1920. During World War II, Spiegle served in the U.S. Navy; he drew for a base newspaper, and painted insignias on fighter and torpedo planes in the South Pacific. After the war, he attended the Chouinard Art Institute in Los Angeles, majoring in illustration. In 1950, Spiegle was selected to create the *Hopalong Cassidy* comic strip, which went on to appear in some 200 newspapers across the country. Spiegle joined Western Publishing in 1956, where he adapted a number of Disney movies and television shows. His credits include *Maverick, Lawman, Rifleman, Rawhide, Spin and Marty, Sea Hunt, Green Hornet,* and *Space Family Robinson,* the inspiration for the television series *Lost in Space.*

Steven Grant was born in Madison, Wisconsin, in 1953. He graduated from the University of Wisconsin, where he studied communication arts and comparative mythology. Grant's comics credits include *Twilight Man, Whisper, Punisher,* and *Life of Pope John Paul II.* The former editor-in-chief of the *Velvet Light Trap Review of Cinema,* Grant has written music criticism for *Trouser Press,* and has contributed to several books on popular culture, including *Close-Ups* and *The Rock Yearbook.* He also has written a variety of widely praised young-adult adventure novels.

YOU'LL NEED A GUIDE FOR LIFE'S GREATEST ADVENTURES!

Unbeatable reference books—exciting, easy-to-use, and always at the head of the class!

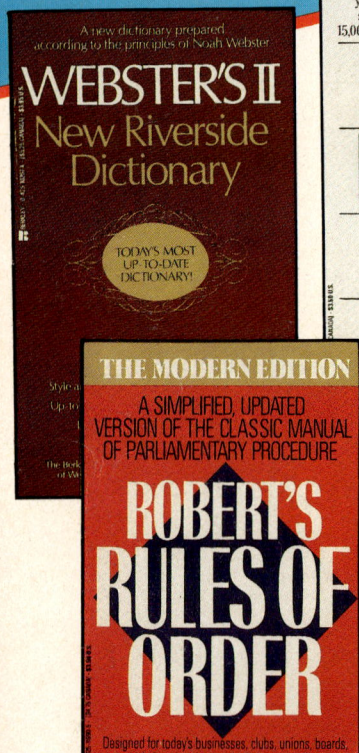
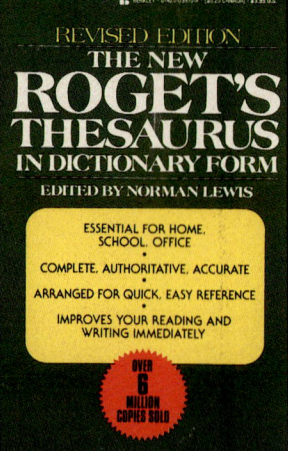
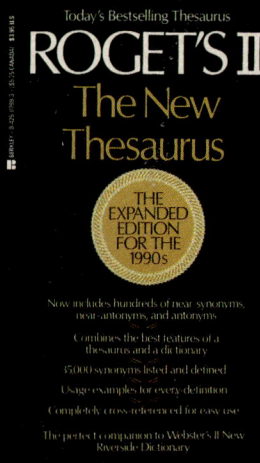

WEBSTER'S II NEW RIVERSIDE DICTIONARY
The original #1 dictionary.

PRIMARY DICTIONARY *(Vol. 1-4)*
Remarkably easy-to-use and filled with handy learning aids.

THE AMERICAN HERITAGE LAROUSSE SPANISH DICTIONARY
Features 70,000 words and phrases from all Spanish American countries.

ROBERT'S RULES OF ORDER *(Modern edition)*
Learn how to run meetings, with the time-honored classic manual for parliamentary procedure.

THE NEW ROGET'S THESAURUS IN DICTIONARY FORM
Authoritative, practical, and efficient, this is today's most popular word-finding book.

ROGET'S II THE NEW THESAURUS *(Expanded edition)*
Now has more information than ever before with 35,000 synonyms listed and defined.

THE BERKLEY PUBLISHING GROUP

Available wherever paperbacks are sold.